ALUN IN THE ATTIC

PROFESSOR MARVO COMES TO TOWN

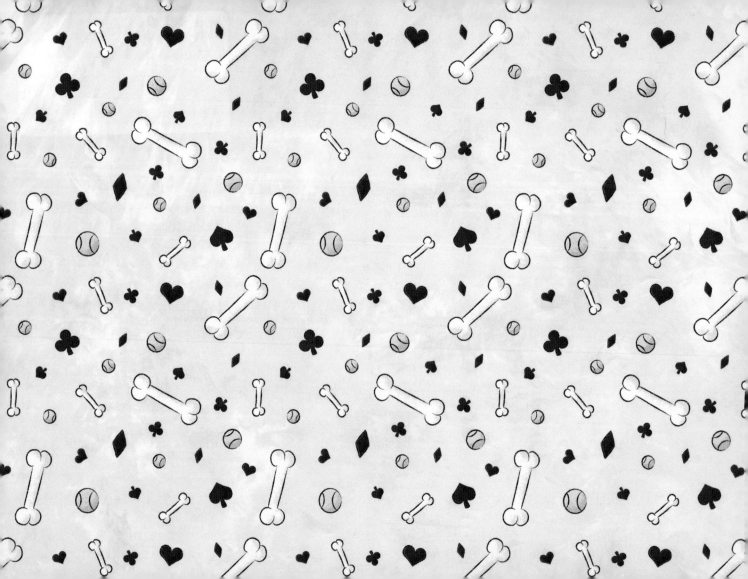

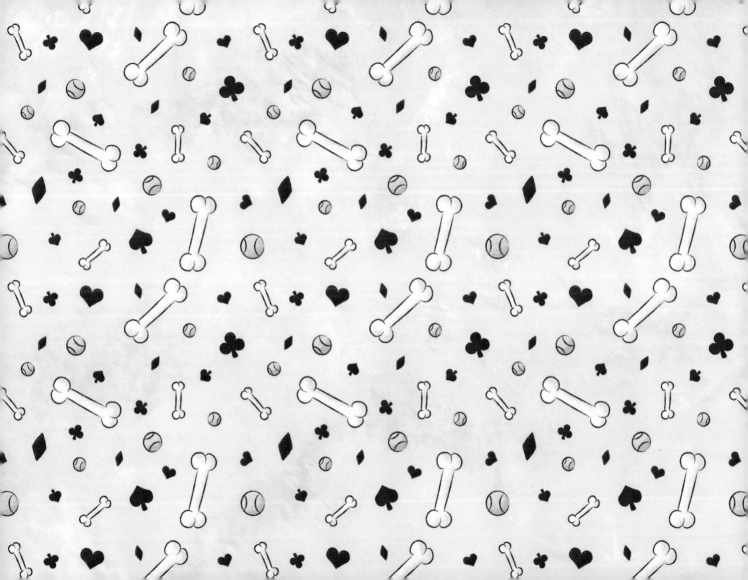

FOR OWEN

ALUN IN THE ATTIC

PROFESSOR MARVO COMES TO TOWN

It was a dark, wet and windy December day. Alun the dog was BORED.

He had tried EVERYTHING to amuse himself ...

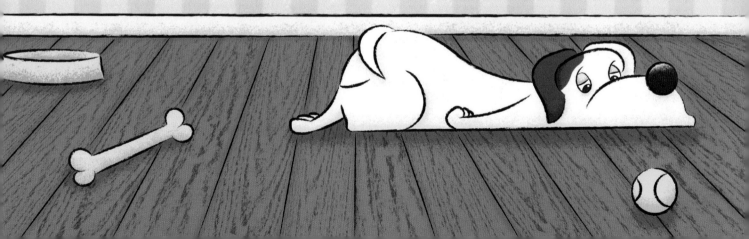

... he had licked his bone until ALL of the taste had GONE ...

... he had dug **SO** many holes in the garden that there
was **NOWHERE** else to dig!

Alun was SO bored, he even hid his FAVOURITE BONE
to see if he could find it again.

Alun had BARKED at Mrs Pomphrey's cat ...

WOOF!

... sending it flying to the TOP of the GIANT OAK TREE!

Normally this made him giggle, but today it was just BORING.

NOTHING was new or exciting.

Alun decided he would go EXPLORING!

He climbed the stairs up to the first floor where a **STRANGE SMELL** went up his nose ...

... and higher still to the second floor, past the **ENORMOUS** cupboard **FULL** of clothes ...

...where NOBODY goes.

Alun pushed the door with a gentle paw.

It opened with an **EERIE** creak. The smell of old books and toys filled the air.

Alun put one paw forward onto the dusty floor and crept underneath a giant cobweb that was hanging from an old rocking chair.

HIDDEN in the corner, under an old tartan blanket ...

... something SHINY caught his eye.

Alun **SLOWLY** pulled back the blanket to find an
OLD WOODEN TRUNK with a mirror on the top.

Written on the side in ancient writing were the words ...

OOOHH!

PROFESSOR MARVO'S
MAGICAL SHOW

PROFESSOR

MAGICAL

Alun carefully opened the box with his left paw and peeked inside.

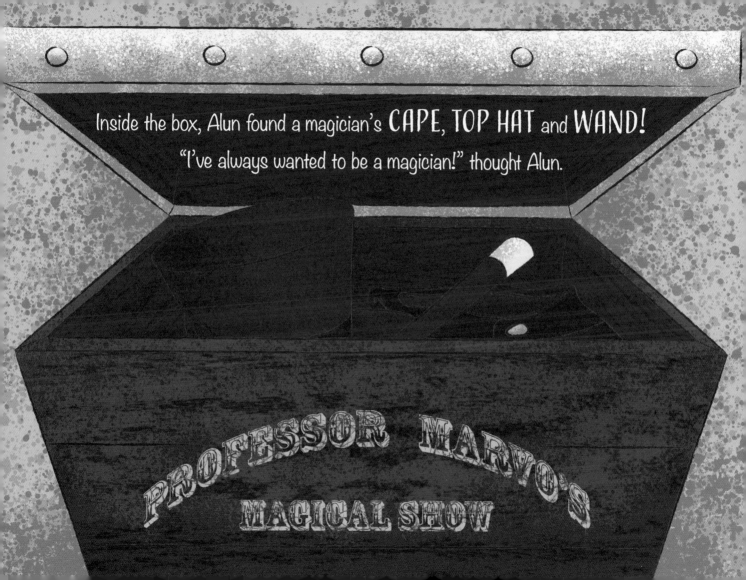

Inside the box, Alun found a magician's CAPE, TOP HAT and WAND!

"I've always wanted to be a magician!" thought Alun.

PROFESSOR MARVO'S
MAGICAL SHOW

He put the **TOP HAT** over his ears ...

... he swept the **CAPE** around his shoulders ...

... and firmly grasped the **WAND** with his paw.

In an instant the attic DISAPPEARED!

Suddenly, Alun found himself in the centre of a **CIRCUS RING**!
The crowd cheered and applauded as a tall, rosy faced
Ringmaster walked up to the microphone.

INTRODUCING
PROFESSOR
MARVO

ONE NIGHT
ONLY!

"Ladies and gentlemen," bellowed the Ringmaster, "now for an act that will MYSTIFY, THRILL and AMAZE you, with a magical expertise that is second to none! May I introduce the WONDERFUL, the FANTABULOUS, the INCREDIBLE ... PROFESSOR MARVO!"

The crowd ROARED as Alun
stepped into the spotlight.

Alun could not believe
that the crowd thought that he was
PROFESSOR MARVO!

TA DA!

Not being one to disappoint, Alun decided that for his first trick, he would SAW a woman in half!

He asked the audience for a volunteer. A tall, blonde lady threw both hands in the air.

Alun instructed her to lie down in the long box in the middle of the ring. He closed the lid, leaving just her FEET hanging out of one end and her HEAD out of the other.

With a **SWISH** of his wand, a **GIANT SAW** appeared!
The audience **GULPED** as Alun drew the saw
back and sank it into the centre of the box.

With a few short strokes,
Alun had cut the box in **TWO!**

With a flourish, Alun turned the boxes around, so that the lady's FEET were pointing at her HEAD!

The blonde woman wiggled her toes and smiled to the crowd (much to Alun's relief)!

With another flick of his magic wand,
a set of SWORDS appeared!

The swords were INCREDIBLY SHARP,
so Alun took care not to cut his paws.

He PLUNGED the swords into the
box one at a time until both ends were
filled with steel.

Alun waved his wand and both ends of the box VANISHED in a puff of smoke.

The audience GASPED and fell silent.

Alun gave one final swish of his wand. In a flash, the tall blonde woman reappeared hanging from the TRAPEZE, high up in the big top!

The crowd whistled and clapped as Alun took a bow. He raised his wand to thank the audience and suddenly found himself ...

. . . back in the ATTIC!

Alun placed the top hat, cape and wand back in the box and FIRMLY shut the lid.

He ducked back under the cobweb and CLOSED the attic door behind him. "What an adventure!" thought Alun. "I have never sawn anyone in half before, but that was enough excitement in one day for any dog!"

Alun settled down in front of the fire
and snuggled beside his favourite toy.
"Being a magician is very tiring for a dog!"
thought Alun with a big yawn.

He put a paw over his
eyes and fell fast asleep,
dreaming of his next
adventure.

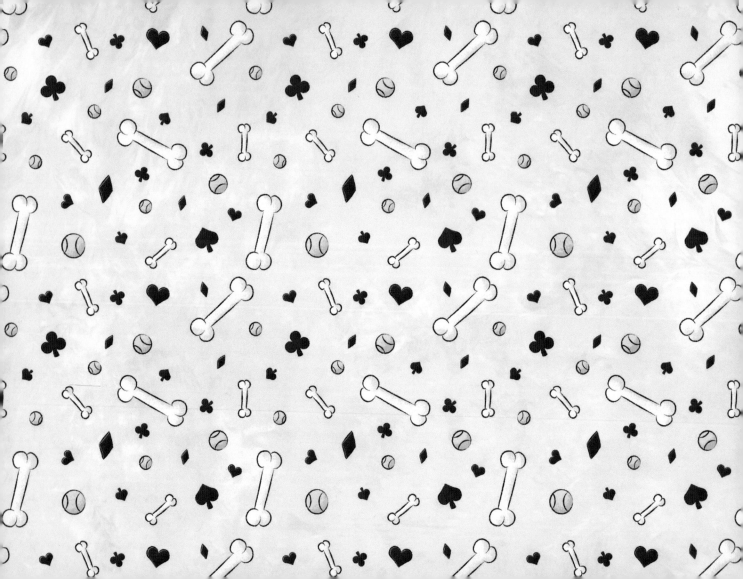

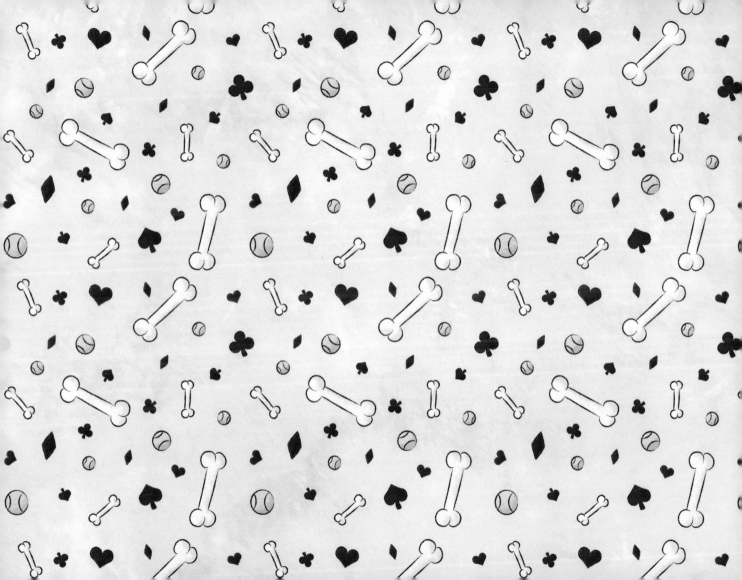

Printed in Great Britain
by Amazon

85478523R00025